THE 9 TASKS OF MISTRY

An Adventure in the
World of Illusion

For Carol

First published in Great Britain by Orchard Books,
96 Leonard Street, London EC2A 4RH

Copyright © 1995 Thumbprint Books Duncan Baird Publishers
Text Copyright © Thumbprint Books
Illustrations © Chris McEwan

ISBN 0-316-55523-1

Library of Congress Catalog Card Number 95-75765

10 9 8 7 6 5 4 3 2 1

First North American Edition

Published simultaneously in Canada
by Little, Brown & Company (Canada) Limited

Printed in China

THE 9 TASKS OF MISTRY

An Adventure
in the World of Illusion

Chris McEwan

There's more than a story to read in this book
There are puzzles to solve - so come, take a look.
Search in the pictures and you can reveal
The secrets they hide and the things they conceal.
If, after trying, you haven't a clue,
Look at the answers on page thirty-two.

LITTLE, BROWN AND COMPANY
BOSTON, NEW YORK, TORONTO, LONDON

FAR, far away, beyond the

misty, murky mountains, where the rainbow ends, lies the World of Illusion. Here the impossible is possible, the unreal is real, and upside down and inside out are downside in and outside up.

This place of enchantment was once ruled by Mistry, Grand Master of Illusion, the most brilliant magician ever known. But even magicians grow old, and in time, Mistry's powers began to fade. He needed someone to take his place, or else all his magic would disappear forever. How could he find a magician who was clever enough to inherit his Cloak of Illusion, the source of all his powers?

Day and night Mistry paced his throne room, working out a test that only the cleverest magician would be able to solve. Then he sent his guards far and wide to pin up his proclamation.

To All Magicians

I Mistry, Grand Master of Illusion, seek a successor. Whoever is the first to complete my Nine Tasks and find his way to my palace shall win the Cloak of Illusion and gain all my powers.

Warning: Those who fail will be imprisoned in the icy Cage of Illusion for twenty years.

Mistry's announcement caused quite a stir, for many magicians longed to go to the World of Illusion and discover its secrets.

One by one, the boldest among them set off to try the Nine Tasks, and one by one, they failed and were trapped in the Cage of Illusion. Soon there was scarcely a magician left to accept Mistry's challenge. Mistry sank into deep despair. Was there not a single magician worthy of his magnificent Cloak?

One day, Whispar, a young
and hopeful magician, came
upon the proclamation. He
was returning home from a long
apprenticeship in the Palace
of Mirrors, far away in the
icy north. Although his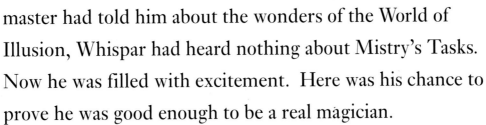
master had told him about the wonders of the World of
Illusion, Whispar had heard nothing about Mistry's Tasks.
Now he was filled with excitement. Here was his chance to
prove he was good enough to be a real magician.

He tucked his little cat, Blink, under his arm and, after
traveling for many days and nights, found a sign at the
Crossroads of Parallel Lines.

A cheery voice called out, "Welcome, welcome. This way to the
Cloak of Illusion . . . or, if you fail, to the *Cage* of Illusion. But
first, young Sir, do you realize the risks you are about to take?"

"I do," replied Whispar nervously, looking all around.
Suddenly, he noticed a face in the gnarled fir tree in front of him.

"Then follow me for Mistry's First Task," creaked the tree.
"And remember, the more you look, the more you'll see. Always
look twice — that's my advice."

Without another word, he strode off across the bridge that led
to the World of Illusion. Whispar and Blink hurried after him.

Task 1 · *Find the secret entrance,*
Where half of the front is also the side
And the space in between is enticingly wide.

Whispar took a deep breath and marched through an opening
that could not possibly exist. There he found a path leading to
an old cottage, where a gardener handed him the Second Task.

Task 2 · *Find every one of Mistry's cats,*
                  Then knock on the door with a rat-a-tat-tat.

Cats can always find cats, so Blink completed the Task in no time. As Whispar called out the answer, the cottage door slowly opened. He gasped in astonishment at the extraordinary city that lay before him.

A flying fish greeted him with the Third Task.

Task 3 · *Find the place where two meets three,*
Where the top is in the air
And the bottom isn't there.

Whispar gulped. It didn't make any sense at all. The fish took him on a flying visit of the city and Whispar looked everywhere twice, but he couldn't see anything that matched the riddle.

"Find a wall that's not a wall," suggested the fish.

Suddenly, Whispar saw the answer in front of him.

13

"Well done, well done," babbled a lively monkey, jumping up as Whispar and Blink entered. "Mistry will be pleased you got this far. Now take the elevator to the umpteenth floor, where you'll come nose to nose with a bossy black rabbit. Hand her this."

The monkey gave Whispar a red envelope, then disappeared in a puff of smoke. Whispar and Blink stepped into the gleaming elevator and zoomed upward.

"About time," sniffed the black rabbit as they stepped out. "Now, tell me what can go faster than the speed of light? What's nothing plus nothing? If the universe didn't exist, what would be in its place?"

Whispar had no idea, so he said nothing.

"Absolutely right!" cried the rabbit. She snatched the envelope and read aloud the Fourth Task upside down.

Task 4.

Look through the keyhole –
Take care you don't fall.
Which musician
Is the tallest of all?

14

Whispar peeped through the keyhole at the six musicians.

"Correct!" boomed the rabbit when Whispar told her the answer.

Whispar squeezed through the tiny keyhole and followed the

musicians down the corridor into a gallery full of peculiar portraits.

"Here's your Fifth Task," said one of the portraits, winking at him.

Task 5 · **There's more to these faces than meets the eye.**
Look every which way as you play I Spy.
When is a horse not a horse?

16

Whispar stared at each portrait, one by one. All of a sudden,
Blink jumped right through one of them and vanished.

"That's it," cried Whispar excitedly.

To his great surprise, a gloved hand reached out and pulled
him straight through the very same picture.

17

Whispar found himself face-to-face with a bearded jester.

"You took a long time to find me," he joked. "Hurry across the river and look for a peddler. He has the answer to the next Task."

With his heart pounding, Whispar set off again. When he reached a bridge over a mile away, a woman leaned out of a window and handed him the Sixth Task and a small key.

> ·Task 6·
> **The key fits the thing**
> **That is not a trick.**
> **Have a good look,**
> **Then take your pick.**

"Show this key to the peddler," she said. "Use it to set free the guide who will lead you to Mistry's palace."

The peddler, on a distant hill, pricked up his ears at the mention of his name. With a hop, he jumped onto the bridge.

"Good morning, evening, and afternoon," he chirped. "Can I interest you in an illusion?"

"Does this key fit something on your tray?" asked Whispar.

"Yes, indeed!" exclaimed the peddler with a knowing wink. "But watch out, my friend — seeing is deceiving."

Whispar rummaged about on the peddler's tray until at last he found something that the key fit. He quickly freed the guide, who led him all the way to Mistry's palace. A stern guard stood at the entrance, barring the way.

"Halt!" he shouted. "No one can enter without solving the Seventh Task."

19

Task 7 · **The battlement steps go around and around,**
But where is the end? Is it up or down?

Whispar studied the steps but couldn't see an end at all.
Then he realized Mistry had set a trick! The answer was easy.
"Well done," said the guard. "You may enter the palace
courtyard and attempt this Eighth Task. Better you than me."

Task 8 · **Can you find the General, Mistry's chief?**
He's the only one in a hat with a leaf.

The courtyard was packed with soldiers all wearing hats.
Whispar's heart sank but he couldn't give up now. He wriggled
through the crowd until, at last, he caught a glimpse of green.
"There's the General," he cried triumphantly.

21

Whispar felt there was nothing he couldn't achieve now.

"Give me Mistry's Final Task," he said grandly to the
General, "so that I may claim the Cloak of Illusion as my own."

The General led him down steps, across ceilings, through
fountains, and up turrets until they reached the closed door to
Mistry's throne room. The General cleared his throat.

24

Task 9 . ***At night I fall on sleepy towns;***
      You can wear me like a gown.
      I go with dagger hand in hand,
      The source of power in all the land.

"Mistry's Last Task is a riddle," said the General solemnly.
"Think hard before you answer this. It's your chance of a lifetime."

The General knocked three times. The door opened, and two
guards led Whispar up to Mistry's throne.

"Well," said Mistry, looking down at him, "what's the answer?"

"Easy," said Whispar, convinced the Cloak was his. "*It's a hat*."

There was a deathly silence. Mistry glared at him furiously.

26

"**Wrong!**" he thundered. "**Completely wrong!** A *hat*? The *hat* of night? *Hat* and dagger? The *Hat* of Illusion? How could it possibly be a hat? The answer, you fool, is a *Cloak*!"

Very slowly, Mistry rose to his feet and pointed a long, thin finger at Whispar. Trembling with terror, Whispar felt the invisible bars of the Cage of Illusion clamp around him.

Mistry towered above him, shaking with rage.

"To become the Grand Master of Illusion, you have to be a strong finisher; otherwise Illusions just crumble into Reality. I had high hopes for you, but now they have vanished into thin air."

Whispar stared miserably at Mistry and his dazzling Cloak. If *only* he could have another chance — just one.

"How long have you been a magician?" demanded Mistry.

"I haven't been one at all yet," whispered Whispar. "I've only just finished my apprenticeship."

"So . . ." Mistry's eyes lit up with delight. "You're not even a proper magician, and yet you have succeeded where every other magician has failed. In that case, I am prepared to make an exceptional exception and give you one final chance."

Mistry clapped his hands, and the bars of the cage slid away.

"Answer these questions, my Tenth and absolutely final Task," proclaimed Mistry, pointing at a large banner, "and the Cloak of Illusion will be yours."

Whispar read the questions carefully. They were as impossible as possible. Mistry handed him a record of his journey so far, and Whispar pored carefully over each page. When he was absolutely sure he knew every answer, he whispered them to Mistry and stood back, holding his breath in anticipation.

· Task 10 ·

- Where does water flow uphill?
- Which of the portraits is both young and old?
- Where do my two watchdogs lie?
- How many faces can you see in the pictures in the portrait gallery?
- Who has a slice of deepest night?
- Where does a green giant look up at the stars?
- Where can you find a rider on a horse?
- Is the chef going up or down the palace steps?

Slowly, very slowly, Mistry untied the knot of his glittering Cloak
and laid it ceremoniously on Whispar's shoulders.

"This is yours," he declared. "You have certainly earned it now."

Whispar grinned proudly at Blink and said nothing as he felt
the weight of the Cloak settle on his young shoulders.

And now the years have passed. Whispar has become old, and he, too, needs a successor. He has sent his guards to pin up this proclamation:

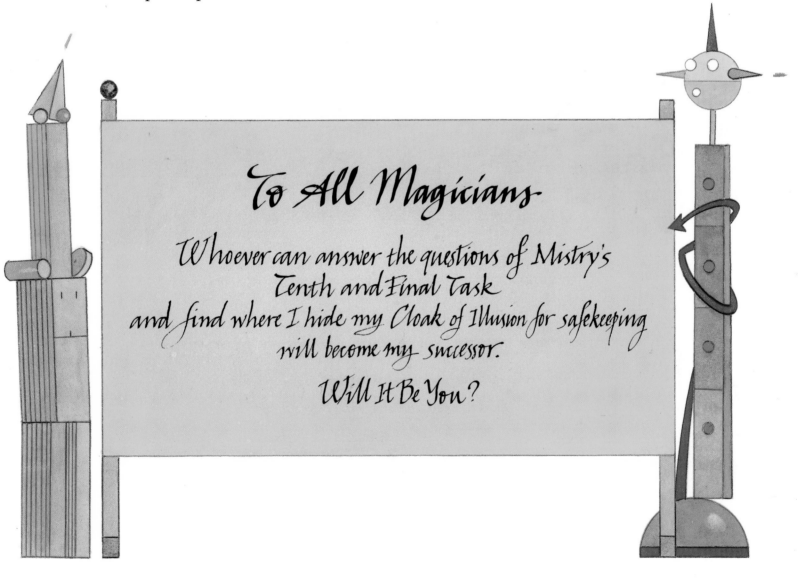

To All Magicians

Whoever can answer the questions of Mistry's
Tenth and Final Task
and find where I hide my Cloak of Illusion for safekeeping
will become my successor.

Will It Be You?

Puzzle

Solutions to the Tasks

Task 1 (page 10)

The secret entrance is the one with the grasshopper on the top on page 10.

Task 2 (page 11)

There are thirty-one cats altogether on page 11.

Task 3 (page 12)

The place is the golden building on page 13.

Task 4 (page 14)

All the musicians on page 15 are exactly the same size.

Task 5 (page 16)

A horse is not a horse when it's a jester, on page 17.

Task 6 (page 19)

The key fits the birdcage on page 19. The guide is the bird.

Task 7 (page 20)

There is no beginning or end to the battlements on page 21.

Task 8 (page 21)

The General is under the flag with the red, blue, and green boxes on page 22.

Task 9 (page 25)

The answer to the General's riddle is a cloak.

Task 10 (page 29)

• Water flows uphill at the mill on page 20.
• The young and old portrait is on the bottom left of page 16.
• The two watchdogs lie on page 4.
• There are 27 faces in the pictures in the portrait gallery on pages 16 and 17.
• The peddler on page 19 has a slice of deepest night.
• The green giant looks up at the stars on page 9.
• The rider and horse are on one of the flags on page 23.
• The chef is going either up or down the palace steps, depending on which way you turn page 24.